Q Quarto Knows

Quarto is the authority on a wide range of topics.

Quarto educates, entertains and enriches the lives of our readers—enthusiasts and lovers of hands-on living.

www.quartoknows.com

For everyone who has ever wanted to be a princess - *M.H.*
To En-Szu, a princess in her own right - *C.v.W & Y-H.H.*

The illustrations in *Princess Grace* are inspired by the original pictures by Caroline Binch for *Amazing Grace* and *Grace and Family*.

First published in Great Britain in 2007 by
Frances Lincoln Children's Books, 74-77 White Lion Street,
London N1 9PF
www.franceslincoln.com

First paperback edition 2007

British Library Cataloguing in Publication Data
available on request

ISBN 978-1-84507-669-6

Illustrated with watercolours

Set in Book Antiqua

Printed by CPI Group (UK) Ltd, Croydon, CR0 4YY

FSC
www.fsc.org

MIX
Paper from
responsible sources
FSC® C013604

Princess Grace

Written by Mary Hoffman

Illustrated by Cornelius van Wright
and Ying-Hwa Hu

F

FRANCES LINCOLN
CHILDREN'S BOOKS

Grace had wanted to be a princess for as long as she could remember.

Most of her favourite stories were about princesses, like Snow White and Sleeping Beauty and the one who couldn't sleep on the pea. Some became princesses with the help of spells, like Cinderella or Beauty.

Grace loved to act out those stories, making
her nana play the fairy godmother or telling
her cat Paw-Paw he had to be the Beast.

So imagine Grace's excitement at school when her teacher
said there would be a competition to choose girls from
her class to be princesses for a day!

"There is going to be a parade with all the local schools,"
said the teacher. "To collect money for charity. And we will
all have a float with a special Queen. Ours has been chosen
already from the top year and it was her idea to pick
two princesses from our class."

Well, after that, all the girls were twirling in
imaginary ballgowns and saying that they were
bound to be the parade princess.

Especially Natalie.

"My Daddy always calls me his princess," she said.
"So I'm used to being one."

This made Grace sad for two reasons. She didn't like
Natalie and she didn't have a daddy of her own.
At least not one who lived with her.

The boys were pretty disgusted with the whole idea.

"Princesses are boring," said Kester.

Grace rushed home, very excited, to tell Ma and Nana the news.

"So can I be a princess, Ma?" she asked. "And will you make me a costume, Nana?"

"Of course, Honey," said Nana. "If you can tell me what a princess wears, I can try to make it."

"And of course you can dress up as a princess, Grace," said Ma. "But that doesn't mean you'll get chosen for the parade."

So Grace rushed off to get out all her storybooks to see if she could find out what princesses wear.

Her best friends Aimee and Maria came round
to help. They didn't want to be princesses
as much as Grace did, because Maria didn't
like being looked at and Aimee
didn't think her mother would
have time to make her a costume.

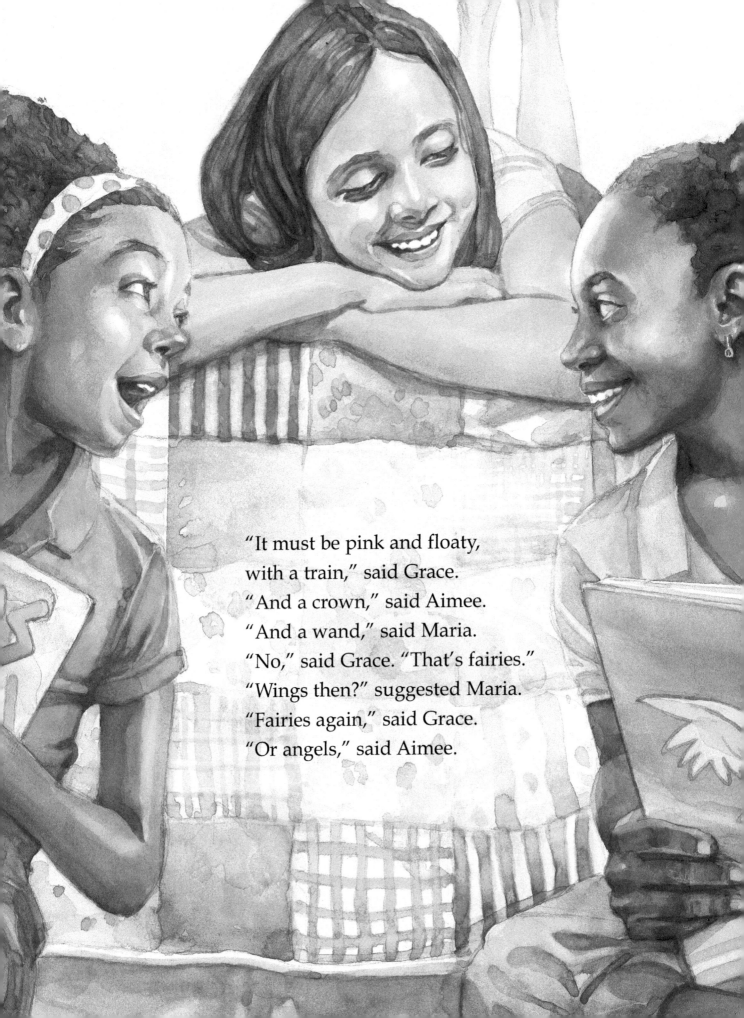

"It must be pink and floaty,
with a train," said Grace.
"And a crown," said Aimee.
"And a wand," said Maria.
"No," said Grace. "That's fairies."
"Wings then?" suggested Maria.
"Fairies again," said Grace.
"Or angels," said Aimee.

"So what am I making?" asked Nana, confused. "I don't know if it's a dress for a Christmas tree fairy or a bridal gown."

"It's a bit like all of those, I think," said Grace.
"Oh I don't know. It must be very pretty."

"There's more than one way to be pretty," said Nana.

"I suppose it depends what she does," said Aimee.

"I don't know," said Grace. "What does a princess do, Nana?"

"You tell me, darling," said Nana.

But nobody could, except for wearing beautiful clothes and looking pretty.

"That doesn't sound so interesting," said Grace. She liked having things to do. "Maybe Kester was right."

"You know what?" said Nana. "I think maybe you've been reading the wrong stories. Why don't you ask your teacher?"

So that's what Grace did.

Her teacher took it very seriously and came back to class with a whole lot of stories about interesting princesses.

There were real ones like Amina of Nigeria, who led warriors into battle and built walls round all the villages,

and Pin-Yang of China, who started a women's army.

"Wow," said Grace, surprised. "They sound more like soldiers than princesses."

"They wouldn't wear anything pretty while they were fighting," said Natalie. "I don't want to be that kind of princess."

But their teacher had found modern princesses too, who were sportswomen or scientists or artists – one had even been a spy!

"That's a bit more like it," said Kester. "You could be one like that, Grace."

Even the story princesses the teacher had found
were not like the ones Grace thought she knew.
There were Cinderellas from Egypt, Cambodia and
the Philippines – and a Zimbabwean girl called Nyasha
who was kind to a snake that turned into a prince.

Grace felt less and less like being the pink and floaty
kind of princess. She couldn't imagine making friends
with a big snake and wearing a sort of fairy costume
at the same time.

"Can't there be princes in the parade?" asked Raj at lunch.
"Why does it have to be just princesses?"
"And why just the pink and pretty sort?" said Grace.
"Can't we have some of these other kinds from other countries?"
"You've changed your tune, Grace," said their teacher.
"I thought you loved fairytale princesses."

"I do," said Grace. "But the others
seem more fun now."
And all the other children agreed.
"Hmn," said the teacher. "I believe
we're going to have to think again
about this parade."

The mums and dads and grannies and childminders
all chatted at the school gates. And the word soon
went around about princes and princesses.

"You need to decide, Grace," said Nana. "Have you
made up your mind what sort of princess you want to be?"

"The kind that has adventures," said Grace.
"And I'd like to be an African one. Is there one from
The Gambia? Can you find me a story?"

"Hold on," said Ma. "Have you been chosen yet?"

"Oh," said Grace. "No, I haven't. I forgot about that."

"No harm in being prepared," said Nana. "Do you know
any Gambian princess stories?"

"You could ring your Papa," said Ma. "He might know."

But Grace's papa didn't know any and nor did his wife Jatou.

"It doesn't matter, Grace," said Nana. "I could use some of that Kente cloth we brought back from The Gambia and make you robes fit for a princess."

"It won't be pink," said Ma. "Will you still like it, Grace?"

"There's more than one way of being pretty," said Grace.

On the day of the parade Grace's school had
the most interesting float of all. But it was
a bit crowded because of all the Japanese
and African and Spanish princes and princesses.
The whole class had been chosen to take part.
Maria didn't mind being looked at because
she wasn't the only one, and Nana
had made a dress for Aimee too.

Raj was a Hindu prince and Kester
was a sort of English knight. Natalie
was like a Christmas tree fairy in
a pink and floaty dress.

But Grace didn't want to be that kind of princess any more.
She was enjoying her West African Kente robes.

"Are you happy?" called Nana.

"Yes," said Grace. "I feel like a proper princess –
ready for an adventure."

Princesses come in all shapes and sizes.
As well as the traditional European stories, like Sleeping Beauty,
there are many versions of Cinderella:
for example, the Egyptian Rhodopis with her golden slippers,
Abadeha from the Philippines and the Cambodian Princess Angkat.
The story of Nyasha and the snake is most easily found in
John Steptoe's *Mufaro's Beautiful Daughters*.

The real-life princess Amina lived in Zaria (now Nigeria)
in the sixteenth century and Pin-Yang was a princess in China
over a thousand years ago. Princess Noor Inayat Khan of Hyderabad
(now in Andhra Pradesh) was shot by the Germans
in Dachau in World War ll for being a spy in France.

Kente cloth is made by the Asante peoples of Ghana
and the Ewe peoples of Ghana and Togo,
and is the best known of all African textiles.
Asante kente (known as "the cloth of kings"), which Grace wears,
is identified by its dazzling, multicoloured patterns
of geometric shapes and bold designs.

MORE GRACE TITLES FROM
FRANCES LINCOLN CHILDREN'S BOOKS

AMAZING GRACE
Mary Hoffman
Illustrated by Caroline Binch

Grace loves to act out stories, so when there's the chance to play
a part in *Peter Pan*, she longs to play Peter. But her classmates say that
Peter was a boy, and besides, he wasn't black... With the support of
her mother and grandmother, however, Grace soon discovers that
if you set your mind to it, you can do anything you want.

ISBN 978-1-84507-749-5

GRACE & FAMILY
Mary Hoffman
Illustrated by Caroline Binch

For Grace, family means Ma, Nana and a cat called Paw-Paw,
so when Papa invites her to visit him in The Gambia, she dreams
of finding a fairy-tale family straight out of her storybooks.
But, as Nana reminds her, families are what you make them...

ISBN 978-1-84507-750-1

STARRING GRACE
Mary Hoffman

Grace the Explorer, Grace the Detective, Grace the Astronaut,
Grace the Doctor... In this collection of eight stories, high-spirited
Grace joins her friends Aimee, Kester, Raj and Maria in a series
of dramatic holiday adventures.
Read more about Grace's adventures in *Bravo, Grace!* and *Encore, Grace!*

ISBN 978-0-7112-2140-6

Frances Lincoln titles are available from all good bookshops.
You can also buy books and find out more about your favourite titles,
authors and illustrators on our website: www.franceslincoln.com